JUST MY SIZE

by May Garelick

pictures by

William Pène du Bois

HARPER & ROW, PUBLISHERS

Just My Size
Text copyright © 1990 by May Garelick
Illustrations copyright © 1990 by William Pène du Bois
Printed in the U.S.A. All rights reserved.
Typography by Andrew Rhodes
1   2   3   4   5   6   7   8   9   10
First Edition

Library of Congress Cataloging-in-Publication Data
Garelick, May, date
    Just my size / by May Garelick ; pictures by William Pène du Bois.
       p.   cm.
    Summary: A little girl reminisces about the beautiful coat she
owned, which as she grew became, in turn, a jacket, a vest and cap, a
knapsack, and finally a beautiful coat for her doll.
    ISBN 0-06-022418-5 : $ — ISBN 0-06-022419-3 (lib. bdg.) : $
    [1. Coats—Fiction.   2. Growth—Fiction.]   I. Du Bois, William
Pène, 1916-   ill. II. Title.
PZ.G17935Ju   1990   89-34513
[E]—dc20   CIP
                                                                  AC

JUST MY SIZE

They bought me a coat.
A beautiful coat
with two big pockets.

I liked my beautiful coat
with the two big pockets.

I wore it on cool days,
on cold and windy days.

On all kinds of days,
I wore it, and wore it.

As I grew taller,
the coat grew shorter.
But still I wore my beautiful coat.

Until, in time,
I outgrew it.

They cut down the coat
and made me a jacket—
just my size.
From the red lining of the coat
they trimmed the jacket.
And with the leftover goods
they made me a wraparound scarf.

I liked my jacket
with the scarf and the pockets.
I liked it—
even more than the coat.

I wore it, and wore it,
and wore it.

Until my arms grew longer,
the sleeves—shorter.

And in time,
I outgrew it.

Then they cut down the jacket
and made me a vest.
A grown-up vest
with the two pockets,
and with yellow-gold buttons.

With the leftover goods
from the jacket,
they made me a cap
to match the vest.

I think I liked the vest the best.
Even more than the jacket.
Even more than the coat.

As I grew wider,
the vest got tighter.
The pockets drooped.
A button popped—
I lost it.

And in time,
I outgrew that vest.

Then they cut down the vest
and made me a knapsack
to wear with my cap.

A knapsack like no other.
With my own name,
with crisscross straps,
with fancy fringes around the edges,
and an extra pocket
for my favorite doll.

I liked that knapsack.
I stuffed it with books
and pens and papers.
I wore it, and wore it,
and wore it,
year after year.

I still have that knapsack.
Now battered and worn—
the straps coming loose,
the pocket half torn.

Was that the end
of my beautiful coat?

Not yet.
From the half-torn pocket,
on my knapsack,
they made a little coat
for my doll.
Just exactly like my big coat.
A copy of my favorite coat.
The one I outgrew.

I think I like
doll's coat
the most.

From the scarf I made a sleeping bag
for my doll,
and pinned it together.
Someday I may learn to sew it.
Meantime,
the pins work fine.

Doll still wears the coat
that was made from the pocket
that was on my knapsack

that was made from my vest
that was made from my jacket
that was made from my coat.

I still think about
my beautiful coat
that I outgrew.

25

That's a coat I'll never forget.